peg + cat

PEG'S MESSY ROOM

JENNIFER OXLEY
+ BILLY ARONSON

CANDLEWICK
ENTERTAINMENT

Peg and Cat were about to have
some very special visitors!

Viv, Connie, and Ramone were coming over to see Cat's artwork--a drawing called *The Circles*.

Cat loved drawing circles. He could draw circles all day. "I like drawing rectangles," said Peg. "Love those straight edges."

Peg wanted to color her rectangle with her favorite crayon, Little Bluey. She found Little Green and Little Yellow--but Little Bluey was missing! Peg had a BIG PROBLEM!

Cat hated to see Peg upset. He tore through drawers and shelves, tossing things out of the way, in search of that little blue crayon. Then he charged into the closet and dug out--WOO HOO!--Little Bluey!

Peg hugged Little Bluey. She hugged Cat, too.

PROBLEM SOLVED!

Then Peg looked around. "Noooo!" she said. "My room is sooo messy. And the very special visitors are on their way! We've got a REALLY BIG PROBLEM!"

How would Peg and Cat straighten up this messy room before the guests arrived?

"I know!" said Peg.
"We can SORT! Do you know what sorting is, Cat?"

"No idea," said Cat.

"Sorting is when you separate things based on their size, shape, color, or whatever.
So do you understand sorting now, Cat?"

"Sort of!"

Peg and Cat sorted.

They separated short things from tall things.

They separated big things from small things.

They separated . . .

things that feel soft from things that feel sticky,

things that smell sweet from things that smell icky,

things that are curvy from things that are straight,

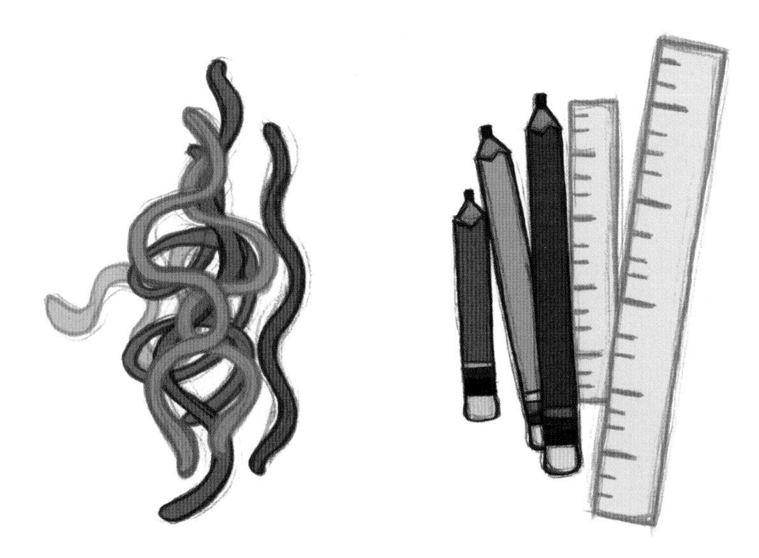

and things that have two legs from things with four legs or eight!

Suddenly they saw triangles spilling out from under the bed. It was the Pig! He was sorting Peg's stuff by shape so he could play with the triangular things.

"I LOVE TRIANGLES!" the Pig sang loudly.

"We know you love triangles, Pig," said Cat.

"My room is just about clean!" said Peg.

But there were still more things to sort!

Peg and Cat quickly sorted them by color.

They separated pink clothes from purple clothes.

They separated green leaves from orange leaves.

They separated brown hats from gray hats.

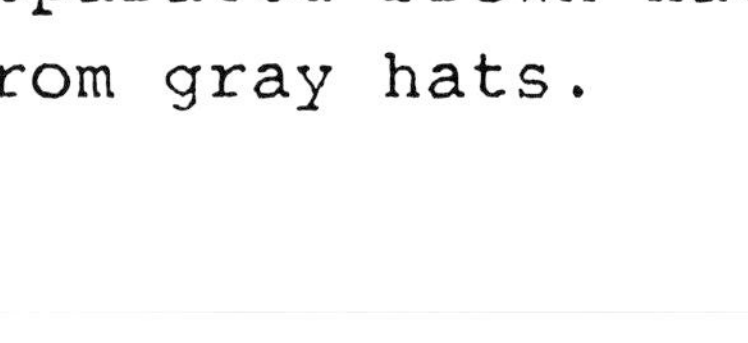

"Hey, Peg!" said Cat.
"What about your underwear with the polka dots?"

Peg giggled. "Hide them in the closet. Fast!"

But when Cat opened the door . . .

. . . out spilled a lot more stuff!
Beach balls and baseballs and records and flying discs!

"I have no idea how to sort all these round things!" said Peg. "And our very special visitors are almost here! I am TOTALLY FREAKING OUT!"

Cat held up his paws, reminding Peg to take a deep breath and count backward from five.

As she counted, Peg noticed Cat holding a beach ball in one hand and a flying disc in the other.

"That's it, you round-thing-sorting Cat!" cried Peg. "We'll sort all those round things into circles, which can lie flat, and spheres, which roll."

Peg's room was totally straightened up. And just in time! The very special visitors arrived to see Cat's drawing, *The Circles*. They gasped, amazed. They'd never seen a work of art that was just circles!

"Cat, why do you like circles so much?" asked Viv.

"I like circles because they're round," he said.

Connie asked Cat if he'd ever draw a square or a rectangle.

"No," said Cat. "That's just not me."

"What about a sphere?" asked Ramone.

"I like my shapes flat," said Cat.

And that was that.

"Who knew that math could help you clean your room?" said famous circle painter Cat.

"PROBLEM SOLVED!" said Peg.

This book is based on the TV series *Peg + Cat.*
Peg + Cat is produced by The Fred Rogers Company.
Created by Jennifer Oxley and Billy Aronson.
Peg's Messy Room is based on a television script by Billy Aronson and background art by Amy De Lay. Art assets assembled by Sarika Matthew.
The PBS KIDS logo is a registered mark of the Public Broadcasting Service and is used with permission.

pbskids.org/peg

First edition 2018

Library of Congress Catalog Card Number pending
ISBN 978-1-5362-0346-2

18 19 20 21 22 23 APS 10 9 8 7 6 5 4 3 2 1

Printed in Humen, Dongguan, China

This book was typeset in OPTITypewriter.
The illustrations were created digitally.

Candlewick Entertainment
an imprint of Candlewick Press
99 Dover Street
Somerville, Massachusetts 02144

visit us at www.candlewick.com